Where's My Bear?

Written by Amy Bray
Illustrated by Maddie Egremont

For Matilda

Where, oh where,
Oh where's my Bear?...

I cannot find him
anywhere!

I've looked high, I've looked low.
Up above and down below.

I've looked inside, I've looked out.
Even on the roundabout.

I have been to all my
favourite places.

Looked inside
the tiniest spaces.

I have retraced
all my steps.

Been to all the
darkest depths.

He's not in the park, or up the tree.
I'm sure he's really missing me.

He could be...
On a boat in the ocean.
On a train, in locomotion.

On an aeroplane,
in the sky.

Watching all the
birds fly by.

At the zoo, where lions roar!
Helping with the keepers' chores.

In a rocket,
floating through space.
To a wondrous alien place.

Where, oh where, Oh where's my Bear?...
I cannot find him anywhere!

I even looked inside the bath,
which really made my mother laugh.

But now it's getting really late
and my tired eyes just cannot wait.

I am still looking in my room,
as it is bedtime very soon.
Where, oh where, oh where's my bear?

Oh look! I found him!
He is there,
sitting in my
reading chair!

What a busy day
it's been
and what a lot
that we have seen.

Now we are tucked up nice and tight.
It is time for us to say goodnight.

Published in 2019 by:
Britain's Next Bestseller
An imprint of Live It Ventures LTD
126 Kirkleatham Lane,
Redcar. Cleveland.
TS10 5DD
www.bnbsbooks.co.uk

Cover design by Maddie Egremont
ISBN: 978-1-910565-98-8

Printed in the U.K

45099735R00016

Printed in Poland
by Amazon Fulfillment
Poland Sp. z o.o., Wrocław